Picking Ap & Pumpkins

by Amy and Richard Hutchings
Photographs by Richard Hutchings

Cartwheel
·B·O·O·K·S·®

SCHOLASTIC INC.
New York Toronto London Auckland Sydney
Mexico City New Delhi Hong Kong Buenos Aires

To Our Sister Jeanne Hundhausen

We wish to thank the Hartman family: Mom, Dad, Grandma, and Kelly and her younger sister, Kristy. We also wish to thank Nina Pacinella and Michael Puleo who worked so hard eating all those apples and carrying those heavy pumpkins.

Without question, this book would not have happened without the enthusiastic cooperation of Scott and Lisa Applegate at Battleview Orchards in Freehold, NJ.

And last, but certainly not least, Amy and I wish to thank our friend and editor Nancy Krulik for her patience, her support, and her resilient sense of humor.

ISBN-13: 978-0-590-48456-5   ISBN-10: 0-590-48456-7

40   10 11 12 13 14/0

Printed in the U.S.A.   40

First Scholastic printing, September 1994

Kristy couldn't believe it! The day she had been waiting for had finally arrived! She and her best friends were finally going apple picking!

"Hi. I'm Scott Applegate," said the man who was giving out the baskets. "Welcome to Battleview Orchards."

In no time at all, Kristy, her friends Michael and Nina, her sister, Kelly, her mom and dad, and her grandmother were taking an old-fashioned hayride! Everyone's cheeks glowed in the crisp autumn air.

There were red Macouns and yellow Delicious apples that were ripe for picking.
Kristy wanted to pick both kinds. The kids decided to start with the red ones.

Nina reached an apple
and took a bite.
  Mmmm! That first apple
tasted so sweet!

While Kristy and Nina piled apples in a basket, Grandma checked them to make sure none were bruised. "These will be perfect for my apple pie," she said smiling. "Look up there!" she said to Nina and Kristy.

Michael had climbed all the way to the top of the tree. "There are some great apples up here!" he called down to Kristy and Nina.

This time it was Kristy's turn to climb to the top of the tree and pick apples from the highest branches.

When everyone had picked enough red apples, Kelly and Michael picked up the basket and carried it back to the hay wagon. Scott drove everyone to the yellow Delicious apple trees.

After she climbed down, Kristy's father showed her how to use a picker to pick apples that were high up in the trees. A picker is a long stick with a basket at the end of it.

Using the picker made apple picking easier — but climbing the trees was still more fun!

"Lunchtime!" Kristy's mother called out. One by one, the children scrambled down from the trees. They sat on the grass and enjoyed a yummy picnic lunch of turkey sandwiches and juice. They were surprised at how hungry they all were — especially after eating all those apples!

    After lunch, it was time to move on to the pumpkin patch. Kristy had never seen so many pumpkins! There were tiny pumpkins, medium pumpkins, and really big pumpkins, too! Kristy found one pumpkin that was so big, she had to ask Grandma to help her lift it!

The pumpkin patch was
a great place to play!
Kelly, Nina, and Michael
pretended to ride pumpkins!
Kristy tried a little one on
as a hat!

All too soon, it was time to leave the pumpkin patch. Kristy's parents helped the children pile their pumpkins together. Then the kids collapsed in a tired heap!

This time, Scott's hay wagon brought everyone to the farm store. While Kristy's mother paid for the apples and pumpkins, Kristy and her friends looked around. They were amazed by all the delicious things that could be made from apples. There were caramel apples, candy apples, apple jam, apple cake, and apple butter. There were pumpkin pies and breads, too. But Kristy knew that when they got home, Grandma would make the best treat of all — apple pie!

Sure enough, as soon as everyone was cleaned up, Grandma asked, "Who wants to help make an apple pie?"

Of course, everyone did!

While Grandma started to peel and slice the apples, Nina and Kristy mixed flour, water, and shortening together in a big bowl to make the dough for the pie crust. When the dough was ready, the girls rolled it out flat with a rolling pin.

Grandma helped the girls put the dough in a pie pan. Then they piled on the apple slices, and covered the pie with more dough.

When at last the pie was in the oven, Kristy felt sad. Her special day was ending far too quickly!

But Kristy's big day wasn't over yet! Her father had a surprise for her!

"Let's make jack-o'-lanterns," he said.

The children had lots of fun drawing faces on their pumpkins. Kristy's father used a sharp knife to cut off all the pumpkin tops. Michael and Kristy scooped out the seeds. Then Kristy's father followed the patterns to carve out the faces.

That night, after Nina and Michael had gone home, Kristy and her family put candles inside their jack-o'-lanterns and watched them glowing in the darkness.

Finally Kristy and her family had a delicious bedtime snack — homemade apple pie! Kristy smiled. It was the perfect ending for the perfect day.